Remembering Fred Marcellino

**Thanks to Captain George Toomey
and Mike Hickey at Boston Towing
and Transportation**

We're MIGHTY grateful to
Justin Chanda, Joanna Cotler, Blair Dore, Holly McGhee,
Alicia Mikles, Jessica Shulsinger and Ruiko Tokunaga

I'm Mighty! Text copyright © 2003 by Kate McMullan Illustrations copyright © 2003 by Jim McMullan Manufactured in China. All rights reserved. For information address HarperCollins Children's Books, a division of HarperCollins Publishers, 195 Broadway, New York, NY 10007. www.harperchildrens.com Library of Congress Cataloging-in-Publication Data McMullan, Kate. I'm mighty! / Kate & Jim McMullan—1st ed. p. cm. Summary: A little tugboat shows how he can bring big ships into the harbor even though he is small. ISBN 0-06-009290-4 — ISBN 0-06-009291-2 (lib. bdg.) [1. Tugboats—Fiction. 2. Size—Fiction. 3. Ships—Fiction.] I. McMullan, Jim, 1936– , ill. II. Title. PZ7.M47879Im 2003 [E]—dc21 2002007948 Typography by Alicia Mikles
16 17 18 SCP 20 19 18 17
❖ First Edition

DOOPER   CARRYKING II   TUGS

I'M MIGHTY!

KATE & JIM McMULLAN

JOANNA COTLER BOOKS
An Imprint of HarperCollinsPublishers

Hey!

Over here!

Yeah, me, the little guy.

When big ships get to the harbor, they need ME! 'Cause I'm mighty! And I can nudge, bump, butt, shove, ram, push, and pull 'em in. *Here I go.*

Gear check:

Towropes?	Coiled!
Hull?	Strong!
Bumpers?	Bouncy!
Engines?	Purring!
Propellers?	Whirring!
Stacks?	Smokin'!
Whistle?	

TOOT!

Shipshape
and ready to
TUG!

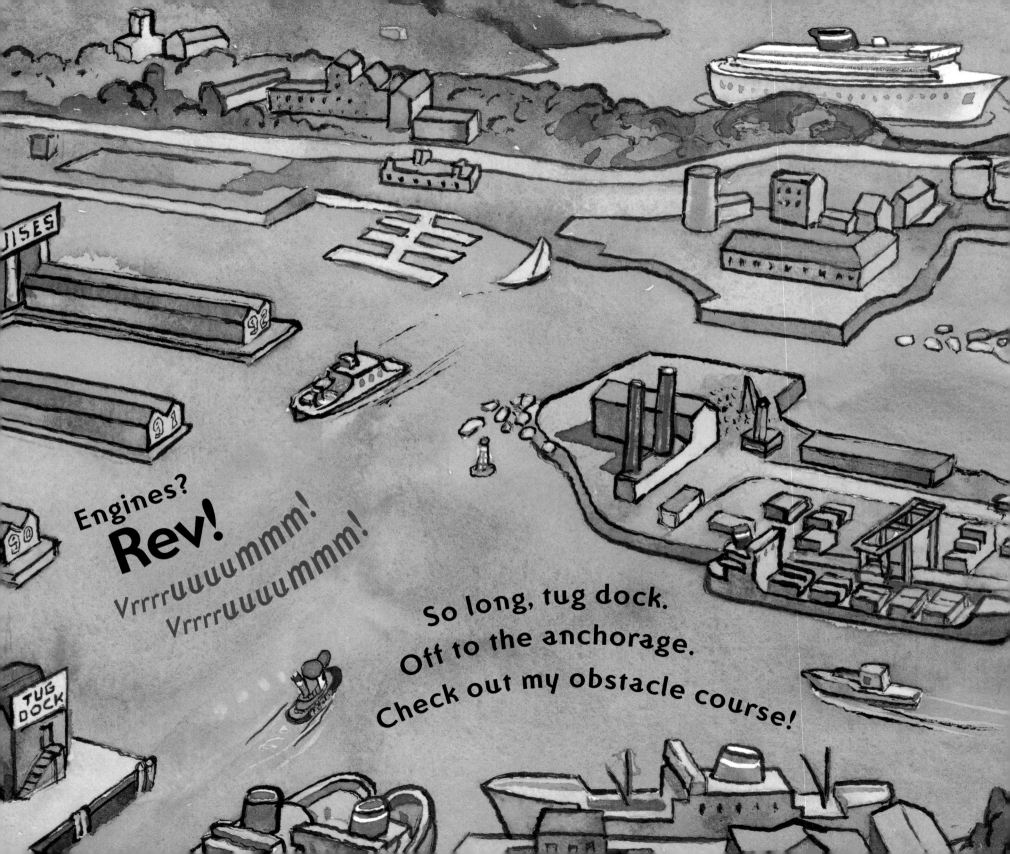

Here's my first tow—
a low-riding tanker
with a belly full of oil.

Coming in too fast, Moby Dee!
PUTTING ON THE BRAKES.

Engines? Reverse!
MmmuuuUrrrrV!
MmmuuuUrrrrV!

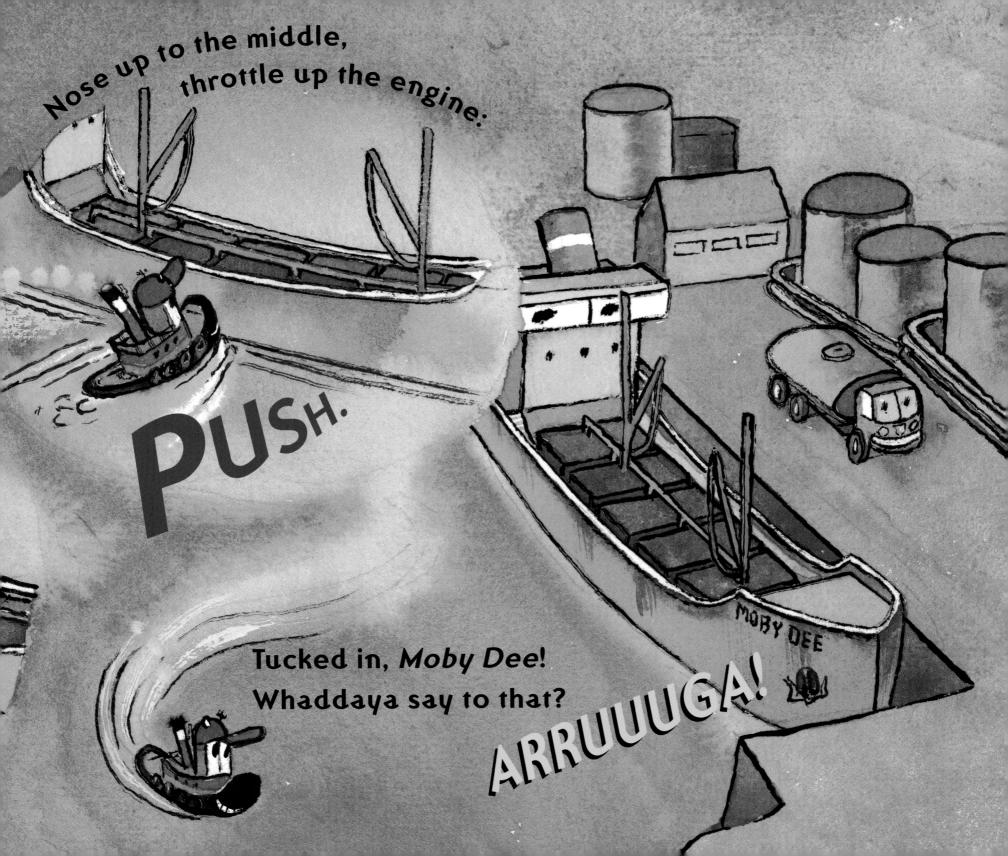

Back to get my next tow—

a six-decker
doozie.

Hey, Carla! Wanna dance?

Round three—
the **Queen Justine,**
a super-duper cruiser,
as **WIDE** as she is long.

*Think this big mama's
got me beat?*
No way!

TOOT, TOOT!

Wide load coming through!
(Pardon me, *Queenie*.)

Let's **TUG!**

Tug.
Tug.
Tug.

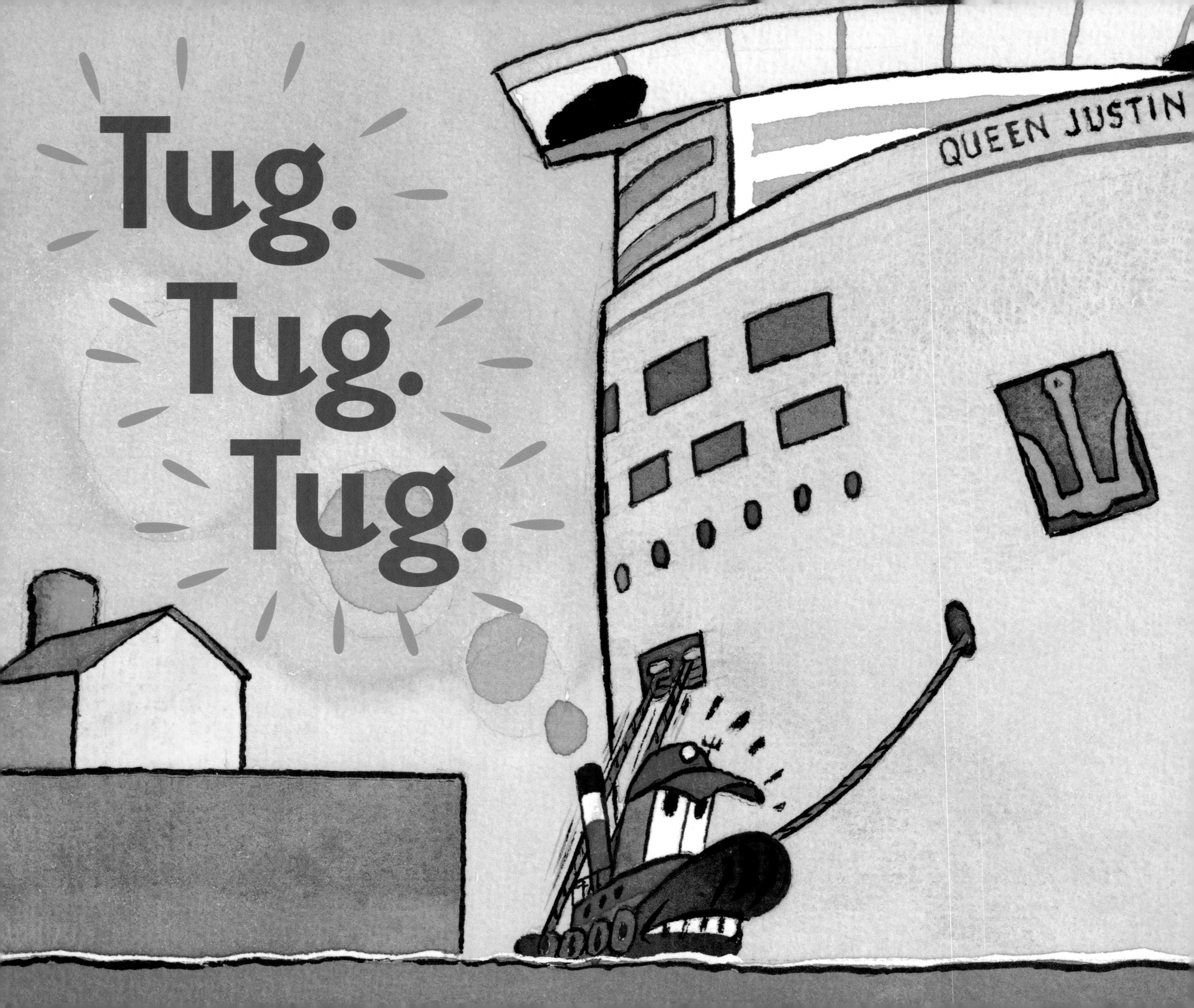

Nothing to it.
Pier 92! This one's for YOU!

**Docked,
yer majesty!**

Yeah! Let's hear it
for the T-boat!

I'm all tuggered out. Back to the barn.

Gear check:

Towropes?	Drying.
Hull?	Dented.
Bumpers?	Bent.
Engines?	Backing.
Propellers?	Slacking.
Stacks?	Empty.
Whistle?	*Toot!*

TUG DOCK

Got to get some shut-eye.

'Cause three **REALLY BIG** ships

are coming in the morning.